Farming Times

Tractor driver
Out of Control
Plows wrong
field

Cows storm through
village

For my lovely, loving daughter Elizabeth T. McGee
and in memory of my grandfather William Earl Broach – MM

To dearest Poppa and the animals he adored – LS

Text copyright © 2004 by Marni McGee
Illustrations copyright © 2004 Leonie Shearing

Published by Bloomsbury, New York and London
Bloomsbury USA Children's Books
175 Fifth Avenue
New York, NY 10010

Library of Congress Cataloging-in-Publication Data
available upon request

ISBN 1-58234-879-0

First U.S. Edition 2004

Printed in China by South China Printing Company, Dongguan, Guangdong

3 5 7 9 10 8 6 4 2

The Noisy Farm

Lots of animal noises to enjoy!

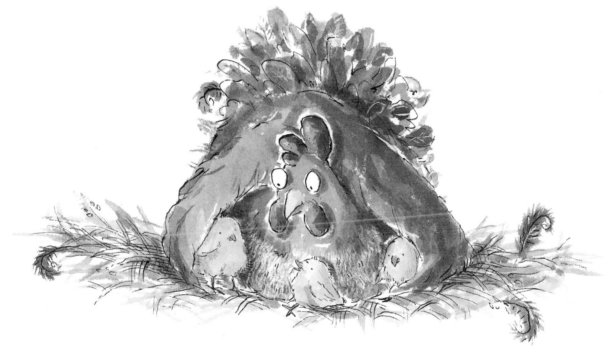

by Marni McGee

illustrated by Leonie Shearing

BLOOMSBURY
CHILDREN'S
BOOKS

In a pocket of earth between two hills
a quiet farmer lives on his land,
far from the bustle of town.
And when, in the morning, the sun first appears,
the rooster begins to crow.
Cock-a-doo, cock-a-doo! Cock-a-doodle-doo!

Cock~a~doodle~doo!

Hearing the rooster's bugle call,
the quiet farmer opens his eyes.

He stretches and gets out of bed.

Squeak!

Squeak go the bedsprings.
Creak goes the floor.

Creak!

Purr-purr
Purr

The yellow cat begins to purr.
Purr-purr. The quiet farmer kneels.
He picks her up and holds her close.

The farmer knows there's work to do.
He dresses and goes outside.
And as he walks down to the barn,
a pail bumps against his knee.
Pong, pong, poink! Pong, pong, poink!

whoo whoo whoo!

Outside an owl is calling, "*Whoo-whoo-whooo!*"
But the farmer does not answer.

His eyes are closed. His breath is deep.
The quiet farmer is fast asleep.

The End